THE
SMALL ONE
A GOOD SAMARITAN

KATHERINE BROWN

ILLUSTRATED BY JESSE CLAY

SCHOLASTIC INC.
New York Toronto London Auckland Sydney
Mexico City New Delhi Hong Kong

ISBN 0-439-04776-5

Copyright © 1998 by Disney Enterprises. All rights reserved.
Published by Scholastic Inc., 555 Broadway, New York, NY 10012,
by arrangement with Disney Press.
SCHOLASTIC and associated logos are trademarks and/or registered trademarks of
Scholastic Inc.

12 11 10 9 8 7 6 5 4 3 2 1   8 9/9 0 1 2 3/0

Printed in the U.S.A.   36

First Scholastic printing, November 1998

The artwork for this book was prepared using watercolor.
This book is set in 14-point Hiroshige Book.

"Love your neighbor as you love yourself."
—Matthew 22:39

"Who is my neighbor?"
—Luke 10:29

There was once a donkey named Small One. He had been loved by a boy who cared very much for him, even though Small One was old and could not do hard work anymore.

The boy had sold Small One to a kind man. The man used the donkey to carry a pregnant woman to Bethlehem for the census-taking. There, the couple had a baby in a stable, because there were no rooms at the inn. The man's name was Joseph, and the woman's name was Mary. They named the baby Jesus.

Jesus and his parents kept Small One, even though he was old and weak. Small One stayed most of the day in the yard, and the little one named Jesus would often play with him.

One day Small One wandered away from the house and the stable, away from the noisy chickens and the bleating sheep. He was looking for a quiet place to rest.

No one noticed that the little old donkey had left.

Small One kept wandering. Soon he came to a steep and rocky hill. He stumbled and fell, rolling down the hill until he stopped. His frail body tumbled into an awkward heap.

He was cut and bruised. One of his legs was twisted under him.
Small One closed his eyes.

The boy was walking on the road from Jerusalem to Jericho. He was older now. He was going to sell some valuables for his father and was carrying them inside his robes. His father had warned him about thieves who might attack the boy and rob him, so the boy looked anxiously about him as he walked.

Then at the bottom of the next hill, the boy saw the little donkey.

Could it be? The boy ran down the hill. "Small One!" he exclaimed.

There was his old friend, crumpled in a small heap, cut and bruised. Tears came to the boy's eyes. How could he help his friend?

The boy looked up and saw a figure on the horizon. Here was someone who could help them!

The figure came closer. It was a priest—surely he would help. "Holy One! This animal is badly hurt. Can you please help me?"

The priest spoke quickly. "That animal is better off finding peace in death. There is nothing you can do for an old, sick donkey. Better just leave him there."

The priest hurried off, leaving the boy and Small One.

The boy could not leave Small One. He could not let him die by the side of the road, all by himself. He hoped that someone would help him move the old donkey to a place where he could get better.

Another figure appeared at the top of the hill. Again, the boy implored, "Please, this animal is badly hurt. Can you help me?"

The man barely glanced their way. He passed to the other side of the road, as far away as possible.

Another figure appeared at the top of the hill. This one had a young, strong donkey with him. They walked carefully down the rocky hill and stopped by the side of Small One.

"This old donkey is badly hurt. Can you help him?" asked the boy again.

The man looked at the boy. There was kindness in his eyes. He could tell that the boy was upset about the old donkey.

"What would you have me do for this animal?" asked the man. "He is very old, and he looks badly injured."

"Do you have anything that we can use to clean his wounds?" asked the boy.

"Yes," said the man. He took a jug of wine and a jug of oil from the bags on his donkey. Then he used the wine and the oil to clean the Small One's cuts, and bandaged his leg with a stick and some linen.

"What should we do now?" said the man.

The boy was quiet. He knew that the man had been very generous, and he hesitated to ask him for more.

"Do you think you could bring Small One to an inn, where he could get better?" the boy asked. "I cannot leave him by the side of the road."

The man replied, "Let us figure out a way."

Together, the boy and the man fixed up a blanket with some sticks, and gently lifted Small One onto it. In this way they were able to drag the little donkey to an inn.

When they reached the inn, the man helped the boy settle Small One in the stable.

Before he left, he gave the boy two silver coins. "Take care of your old friend," he said.

"Wait!" said the boy. "Tell me your name! Where are you from?"

"My name does not matter," said the man. "I am from Samaria."

"Thank you for your kindness," said the boy. "Small One and I will never forget it."

The next day, Joseph arrived at the inn. He saw Small One in the stable yard, limping about with the splint on his leg. The boy sat nearby.

"Small One!" exclaimed Joseph. "I found you!"

The boy explained what had happened to Small One. He told Joseph about the strangers who would not help, and about the stranger who did.

"That is a good story," said Joseph. "I will tell that story to my son, who will be so happy to see Small One. We will call the man who helped, 'The Good Samaritan.'"

The boy gave Small One a hug. He knew that his old friend would get better again with his family. He climbed high atop the wall of the inn to wave good-bye to Small One once again, as he hobbled off with Joseph to his home.